PHOTOGRAPHS BY

JEFFREY JAY FOXX

ANGELA
WEAVES
A
DREAM

TEXT BY MICHÈLE SOLÁ

HYPERION BOOKS FOR CHILDREN
NEW YORK

Angela ran to meet her friends in the central square of San Andrés, a mountain village in southern Mexico. Her bare feet flew over the dirt street, and her long braid bounced on her back. She had spent one whole year preparing for the Weaving Contest. Today was the day and she was ready!

In the past, only older girls and women were allowed to enter the contest. But last summer the judges made an announcement that still made Angela's hands shake with excitement: Next year, there would be a new prize for beginners, a First Sampler Prize awarded to the best first weaving.

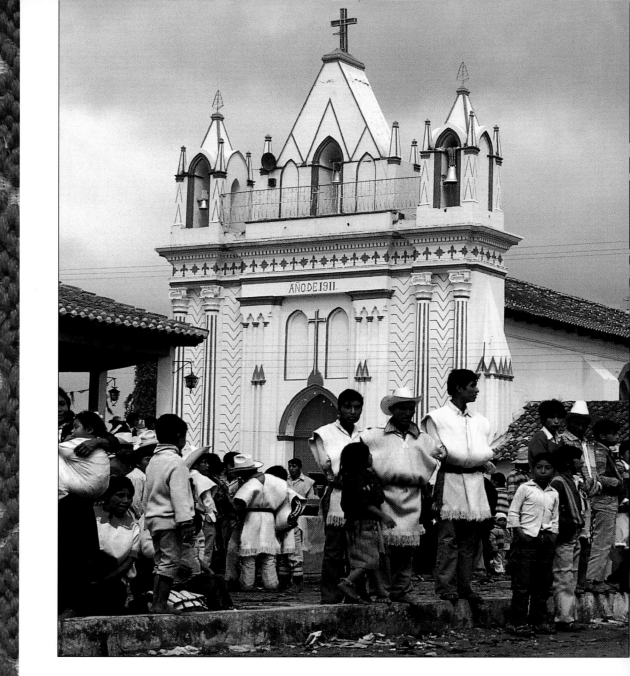

As trucks full of villagers from nearby towns began arriving in San Andrés, Angela peered into the crowd, watching for friends she saw only once or twice a year. The women and girls came dressed in their finest handwoven clothes—a decorated cotton blouse called a *huipil* and a long dark blue skirt pleated at the waist and held in place by a maroon sash. The men and boys sported their best hats and wore heavy woven tunics over homespun pants.

Angela prided herself on how quickly she could identify people's villages by what they wore—women wearing diamond-brocade huipils with deep maroon wool designs were from Tenejapa; bright blue polyester blouses with white-flowered ribbons were from Chamula; and pale pink shawls embroidered with flowers were from Zinacantán. Men wearing black tunics and straw hats with streaming, colorful ribbons were from Tenejapa, and those with thick white tunics were from Chamula.

Voices coming from the Weavers' House caught Angela's attention. She could see a group of young girls surrounding Abuelita, her grandmother, one of the master weavers of Chiapas. Angela knew that storytelling would soon begin. Wherever Abuelita went, less experienced weavers stopped what they were doing to hear what she had to say. Angela hurried to join the group of girls now sitting around Abuelita in the grass, getting there just in time to hear the first words of the story. It was one of many that Abuelita's own mother had told her when she first showed an interest in weaving.

The plazas of Maya villages are the center of the town. Each week they become open-air markets offering fruits, vegetables, and other foods as well as clothing, tools, and household items.

The dominant feature of a village's main plaza is the Catholic church. Weavers and their families who live a distance from the village and cannot attend church regularly take the time while in town to spend a few minutes there praying.

In the beginning, it is said, there was only the sea and the sky, and the world was completely silent. The gods of both the sea and sky were named Xpiyacoc and Xmucane. One day they came together and broke the silence.

"Let the waters part," said one.

"Let there be light," said the other.

"Let great mountains rise from the sea," they said in unison.

As soon as the words were spoken, the waters parted, dawn broke on the horizon, and mountains arose in the middle of the sea. Between the mountains, foaming rivers flowed in the valleys. Along the water's edge, great forests grew. From that time forward, these gods became known as the Creator Gods.

The gods followed the advice of Xpiyacoc and Xmucane, the great-grandparent gods, as they created the Ancestors to watch over the new world. First the gods modeled them out of clay, but the rains came and the Ancestors dissolved into mud. Next the gods carved them from wood, but the rains came again and the Ancestors rotted away. Finally the Gods shaped them from corn, and when the rains came the Ancestors grew tall and strong. The gods were happy and the Ancestors have been known as Earth Mother and Earth Father ever since.

Xpiyacoc and Xmucane then created villages and people to inhabit them. To each village they assigned a sacred mountain, a weavers' saint, and a set of seven sacred weaving designs. The ancestor gods also gave the villagers instructions about how to keep

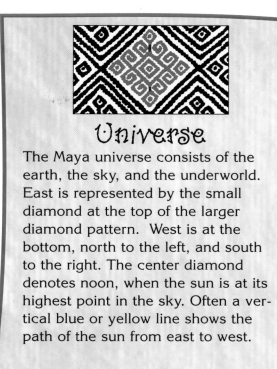

Universe

The Maya universe consists of the earth, the sky, and the underworld. East is represented by the small diamond at the top of the larger diamond pattern. West is at the bottom, north to the left, and south to the right. The center diamond denotes noon, when the sun is at its highest point in the sky. Often a vertical blue or yellow line shows the path of the sun from east to west.

the Maya world strong and peaceful. Xpiyacoc taught them how to plant corn and make tortillas. Xmucane taught the women how to weave stories into cotton cloth by combining the sacred designs in unique patterns.

The weavers' saint assured the gods she would pass on the secrets of the sacred designs to each new girl born into a village. Young girls would practice the yarn designs by weaving them one at a time into cotton samplers. Later they would weave more intricate samplers by combining designs, and eventually they would weave their first huipil. If the villagers forgot the meanings of the designs or how to combine them properly, the saint promised to refresh their memories through their dreams.

Although Angela often weaves alone, she sometimes joins other girls her age at the Weavers' House. There they set up their looms and practice together.

Angela had heard this story many times. As Abuelita told it again, Angela thought back over the past year. For twelve months, Angela and all the girls of San Andrés had spent hours at their looms, determined to have their first samplers ready. But they had really begun preparing for this day years before.

When she was no more than three years old, Angela had learned to card wool. Abuelita taught her to use tiny combs with pointed teeth to brush away the bits of straw and clumps of dirt stuck in the fibers. The carded wool was then set aside to be spun into yarn.

In the years that followed, Angela accompanied Abuelita to the pastures in the mountains to help tend the family's sheep. While Abuelita kept her eyes on the animals, her hands were busy with her spindle. Angela begged so often for one of her own that one morning Abuelita fashioned a crude spindle for her out of a stick pressed into a ball of clay. At first Angela just wrapped the wool around the stick, but gradually she learned to twirl the spindle faster and faster. Her first yarn was all lumpy and full of knots, but the more she practiced the better she spun. Angela eventually graduated to using a full-size spindle like her grandmother's, bought at the market.

(Above) Just as Abuelita taught Angela, another master weaver of San Andrés is teaching her granddaughter to card wool. She gives her small clumps of wool and two handmade wire combs. As the girl combs the wool fibers over and over, bits of dirt fall to the ground, leaving clean tufts ready to be spun into yarn.

(Right) Although Maya women have been weavers since ancient times, they originally wove only cotton. Sheep were first brought to the highlands of Chiapas from Spain in the sixteenth century. Maya weavers quickly began using the wool to produce warm cloth.

Carding and spinning can be done at any time of year, but dyeing cannot. The plants and insects needed for dyeing are available only during the summer months. All the weavers of San Andrés put aside one week each summer to dye yarn together: yellow on Monday, orange on Tuesday, green on Wednesday, blue on Thursday, pink and red on Friday, and black on Saturday.

Early each morning the weavers started a fire and put water to boil in a big earthenware pot. While the water was heating, Angela and the other girls helped collect the dye to be used that day. For the first three days, they gathered the leaves and vines that turned boiling water brilliant shades of yellow, orange, or green. The next two days they harvested tiny insects from cactus plants that produced pink, red, and blue dyes. The last day they collected mud, bark, and stones that would make a deep black.

(Opposite) Spinning wool into yarn requires a spindle, which is made of a smooth, round dowel with a heavy clay ball at one end. A weaver pulls a tuft of the wool and twirls it with her hands until it is long enough to attach to the clean spindle. Then she quickly rotates the spindle inside a ceramic bowl or gourd with one hand. She uses the other hand to stretch and twist the wool fibers together into yarn, which wraps around the spindle into a ball. Rotating the spindle rapidly and stretching the wool evenly are essential to produce yarn of a uniform thickness.

(Above) Pink and red dyes are made by crushing hundreds of small cochineal insects that live on cactus plants and boiling them in water. Before the skeins of yarn are added, the insects are strained with a ceramic sieve. Dye is continuously poured over the yarn to ensure even coloring.

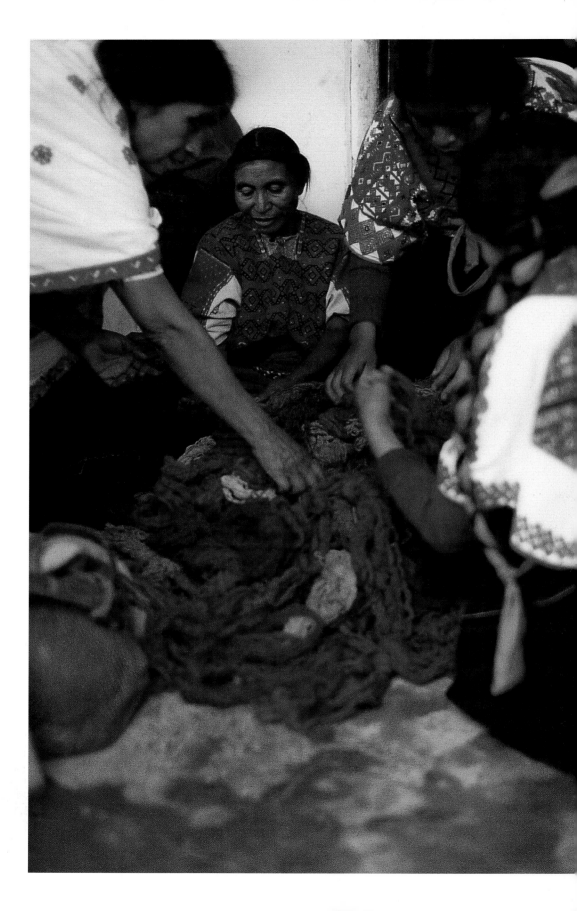

After drying, the yarn skeins are examined closely for flaws or any dirt or dyeing material that may cling to them.

Upon the girls' return from the woods and fields, the master weavers took over. They carefully mixed that day's dye into the boiling water and watched as pale colors became richer. When the water reached the right shade, they dipped the yarn into the pot over and over again. At the end of the week, what had once been a pile of white yarn was transformed into seven soft colors.

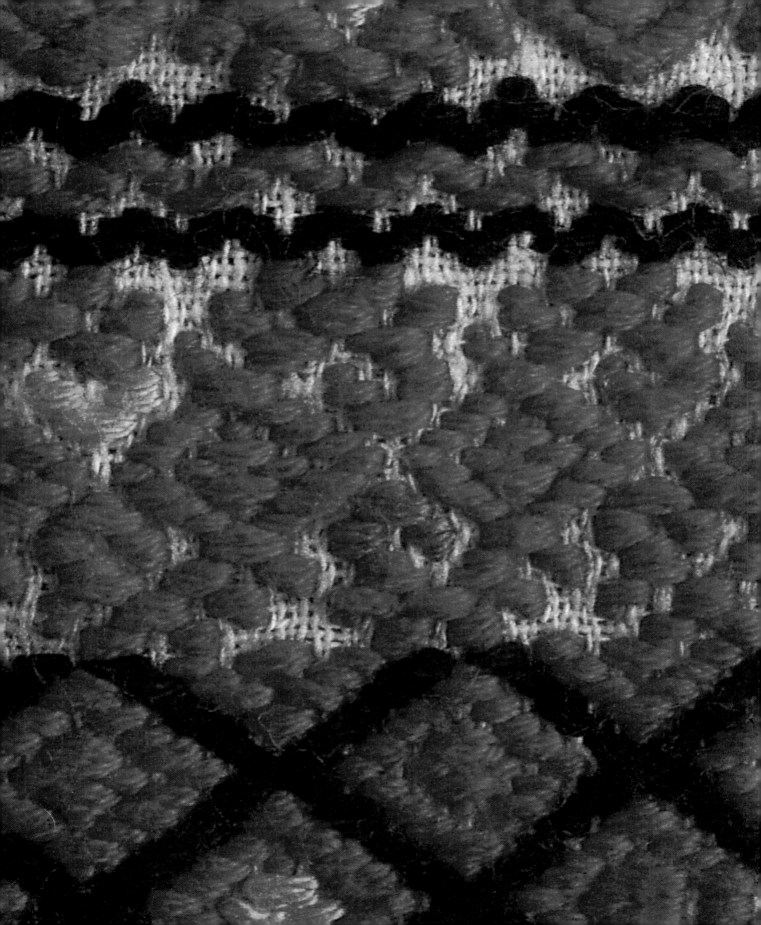

Angela desperately wanted to begin weaving once she could spin and dye yarn well. She and her friends sometimes made pretend looms, tying bundles of sticks together with pieces of discarded cotton thread and yarn. Other times they begged Abuelita to take down her backstrap loom from the peg on the wall, attach one end to a tree, and show them how it worked. Angela memorized the different parts and could name whichever one Abuelita pointed to: the warp, the weft, the shuttle, the heddle, or the batten.

On Angela's eighth birthday, Abuelita announced that Angela was ready to learn the seven sacred weaving designs of San Andrés. Angela was thrilled: to learn the designs took her one step closer to actually weaving!

Scorpion

The scorpion is easily recognized by its long, curling tail. An ancient legend tells that Anhel, the lightning god, was once bitten by the scorpion. As punishment, the scorpion is forever condemned to live under a rock. Every time the scorpion ventures out into an open space, Anhel hurls bolts of lightning at it and produces rain.

THE SEVEN SACRED DESIGNS OF SAN ANDRÉS

Ancestors

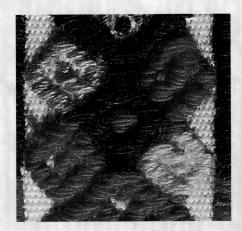

Butterfly

Flowering Corn

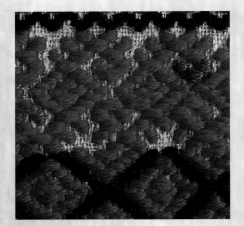

Scorpion

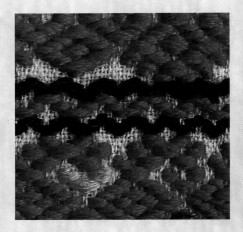

Snake

Toad

Universe

Every village has its own set of designs passed from one generation to the next through ancient Maya stories. Although the colors of the designs and the combinations in which the designs appear can vary, the seven designs remain the same. In Maya tradition, the oldest members of the family pass on these stories. Abuelito, Angela's grandfather, was her teacher.

Angela spent hours with Abuelito in the *milpa*, the family's cornfield, helping him weed. In between rows they would rest and Abuelito would tell her one of the stories.

Abuelito clears the weeds from the family's *milpa*. The Maya sometimes refer to corn as "sacred sunbeams." Every activity involving corn is considered sacred.

17

Long, long ago, Xpiyacoc and Xmucane created the Ancestors. They are called Earth Mother and Earth Father and to this day they watch over San Andrés from their home, the cave, high up in the sacred mountain. They are masters of the wind and the water, the thunder and the rain. They work hand in hand with the scorpions who attract lightning and the toads who sing of oncoming rain to make the earth blossom.

Earth Mother and Earth Father have four daughters who sit at the back of the cave from early morning till late at night, fluffing piles upon piles of cotton. Some piles are shimmering white, others dusty gray. The more the daughters fluff, the higher the piles grow. When every corner of the cave is filled, bits of cotton escape into the sky, forming the clouds that are seen rising over the peak of the sacred mountain. Maya farmers keep a close watch on the clouds from the day they plant their corn until its harvest. When the sun shines and white clouds dot the sky, Earth Mother and Earth Father are warming the corn plants. When the sun is hidden and the sky is filled with gray clouds, the daughters are sending rain to help the corn grow.

Abuelito sometimes tested how well Angela was paying attention by asking her to list the designs—Universe, Butterfly, Ancestors, Toad, Snake,

Ancestors

The Ancestors consist of a pair of figures, the Earth Mother and Earth Father. The Earth Father can be identified by the three thick vertical lines at its center. Although occasionally found alone, more often it appears alongside the Earth Mother, recognizable by its outstretched arms. The Maya believe that the Ancestors live in a cave located in each village's sacred mountain.

Scorpion, and Flowering Corn. Once she could name them perfectly, Abuelito would ask her to retell one of his stories without missing a single detail.

During the months she was learning the stories, Angela and her grandmother went to the village church many times to visit Santa Rosario, the weavers' saint. Abuelita told Angela how the saint would one day visit in her dreams and grant her the vision, skill, and grace she would need to become a weaver. Inside the dark doorway of the church, Angela lit a candle and carried it to the statue of Santa Rosario. She closed her eyes tight and promised she would hang her first sampler on the saint's huipil. Then Angela repeated the weavers' prayer over and over again:

Ak'bun ti oxib ach'ul grasya
Ak'bun ti oxib ach'ul ventisyon
Ti sba yol ajalante'e
Ti sba yol atzutzube
Yu'un la me chak xchan
Yu'un la me chak yich'

Give me three graces
Give me three battens
Give me three heddles
So I may weave my cloth
So I may weave my sampler
So I may one day weave my own huipil.

(Right) Like the other girls her age who yearn to become weavers, Angela frequently visits Santa Rosario to ask for guidance and inspiration.

(Opposite) Angela attaches one end of the loom to a high hook on a post near her house and secures the other end with a wide leather belt around her waist. When weaving with a backstrap loom, Angela controls the tension on the threads by leaning forward and back with her whole torso.

Angela could barely contain her excitement the day Abuelita agreed that she was ready to learn to weave. Abuelita helped her tie one end of her loom to a hook high up on a post and the other end to her waist. Sitting on a stool, Angela practiced rocking gently forward and back, forward and back.

Before attempting the colorful patterns, Angela had to begin by weaving solid white cotton. She struggled at first with passing the shuttle cleanly through the warp threads. Sometimes she pulled the shuttle too tight and the edges of the white cloth rippled. When she tried to weave looser edges, little loops of thread dangled at the end of the row. Abuelita always made Angela take out the mistakes until every edge was straight. Angela was determined and wove inch after inch of white cotton. Months passed.

When Angela's cotton cloth finally met with Abuelita's approval, she was ready to use colored yarns to practice the sacred designs. Abuelita gave her granddaughter a model loom that already had each of the seven colorful designs neatly brocaded in the center of the white cloth. Abuelita taught Angela to count the colored threads and then reproduce the design on her own loom.

(Opposite) Weaving white cloth requires a weaver to alternate passing a shuttle with cotton thread through first the odd and then the even pairs of warp threads. One of the challenges for Angela as a beginner is to achieve a uniform width in the cloth by pulling the shuttle to precisely the same length on every row.

(Right) A backstrap loom consists of many parts. At one end is the cord (a) used to fasten the loom to a tree or post, and at the other is the backstrap (j), usually a leather belt that the weaver attaches behind her back. During the process of setting up the loom, warp threads (b) are wound around the heddles or heald rods (d, e) to keep the threads from tangling. There are two sets of interwoven warps called "odd" and "even" pairs. These are kept separate by the shed roll or shed stick (c). The weft (g) is attached to the shuttle (i). To make cloth (h), the weaver draws the weft thread through the warp threads. After each pass she pulls down the batten (f) to push each row compactly into place to tighten the weave.

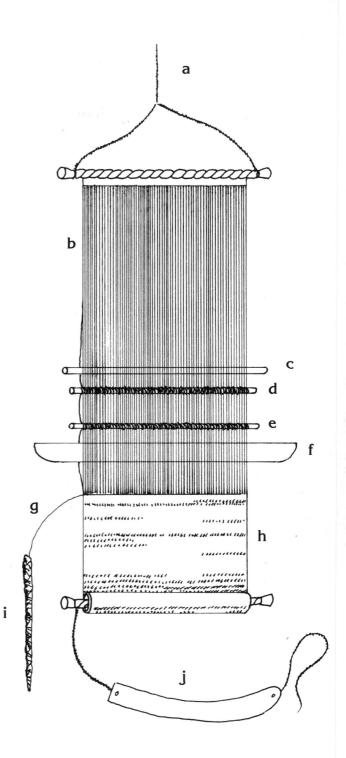

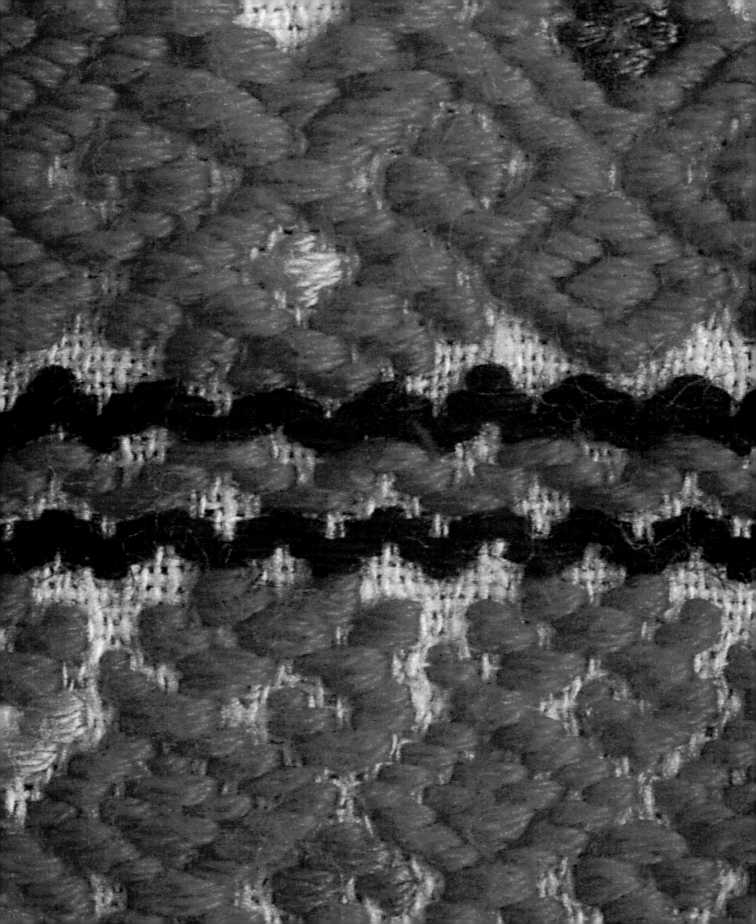

ngela unrolled the first design on Abuelita's model. It was the Snake. In the first row, there was one red stitch, one warp thread wide. In the next row, there was another red stitch, but this one was three warp threads wide. In the following row she counted two over, one under, two over. And so it repeated, until the red threads looked like seven evenly spaced climbing stairs. Proud of being able to count the threads, Angela now tried to weave it herself. Over and over again she practiced, eventually perfecting the first design.

Snake

The snake is a messenger between the earth and the underworld and lives in the cave of the Ancestors. The Snake is found in many forms on Maya weavings—sometimes a simple steplike design, other times as part of the Flowering Corn design.

She then unrolled the second design on the model loom. It was the Toad. Angela especially liked working on this design because she loved the story of Antonia, the toad that guards the Ancestors' cave. For the Maya the sound of a toad's song is a sign that before long the rains will fall and the corn will begin to flower.

One by one, Angela practiced weaving all seven sacred designs. Some days her fingers ached from guiding the colorful yarn through the tight spaces between the white warp threads. Other days her head spun from counting over and under, over and under, first on the model, then on her own loom. When Abuelita found mistakes and made her start over, Angela felt so frustrated she wanted to quit.

Toad

The toad stands guard at the mouth of the Ancestors' cave and watches for signs of approaching rain. When the sky darkens the toad sings, alerting nearby Maya villages that the rain is coming and soon the corn will flower.

Nothing helped her give up pouting faster than her grandfather's offer to tell her one of the design stories again. Abuelito
loved to tell the story of Flowering Corn as he and Angela sat in
the milpa, surrounded by corn on all sides.

(Opposite) Angela likes to spend time with
Abuelito, especially when he stops working
to tell her a story.

(Above) According to Maya legends, each
corner of the universe (east, north, west,
and south) is represented by one of the four
common colors of corn: red, white, black,
and yellow.

ong ago, Xpiyacoc and Xmucane were trying to shape the Ancestors. They asked the fox, the coyote, the parrot, and the crow for advice. The animals thought and thought and came up with a suggestion. "Corn," they said, "will neither melt nor rot in the rain. It comes in as many colors as the sunbeams do. If Xmucane will use corn, then surely the Ancestors and the people created after them will be many beautiful colors, too." So Xmucane gathered some yellow, white, black, and red ears of corn and ground them into cornmeal on her stone metate, just as Maya women do today when they are making tortillas.

When Xmucane finished she had cornmeal that was a mixture of colors and some clear corn broth. She used the meal to shape the flesh and the broth to form the blood of the Ancestors, called Earth Mother and Earth Father. Since that time the Ancestors have watched over Maya villages from their cave. When the cornfields flower, the villagers know that the Ancestors are pleased with them.

Flowering Corn

A symbol of the universe in harmony, this design is sometimes a variation of the Snake design, extending the zigzags into what look like flowers. Or it looks similar to the Earth Mother design, with multiple arms. The Maya believe that just as a corn plant has many branches, the Earth Mother has many arms with which to embrace her children.

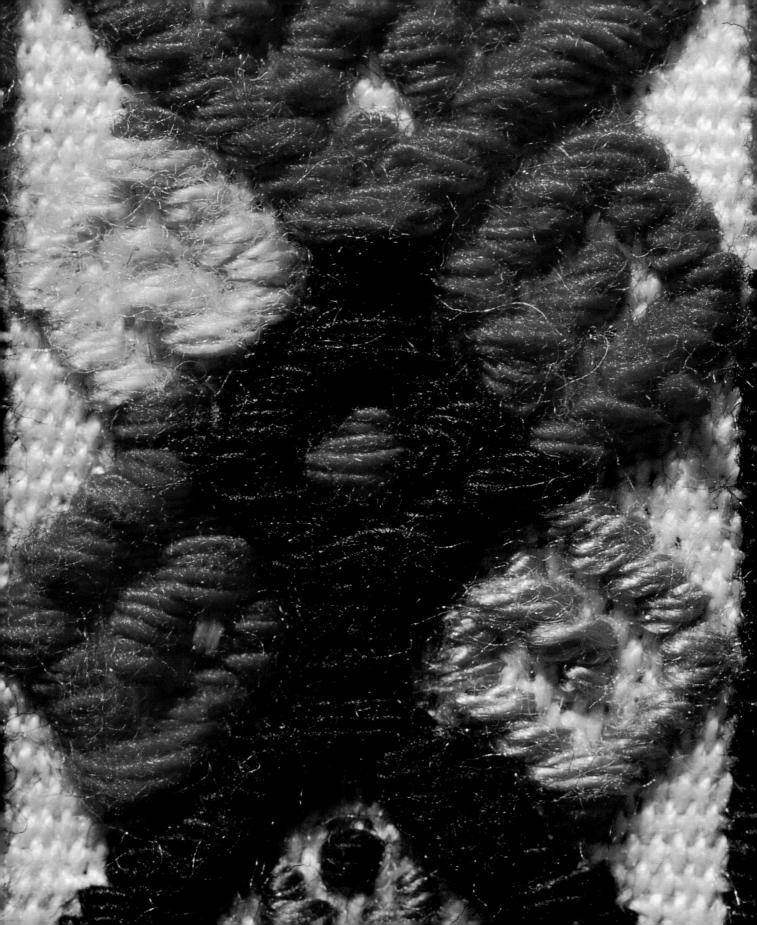

At last the day came when Abuelita couldn't find a single mistake in Angela's designs. Not long afterward, Angela learned of the new First Sampler Prize and asked her grandmother when she would be allowed to create her own design and weave her first sampler. Abuelita checked Angela's most recent weaving very carefully. Satisfied, she reminded Angela that to weave a sampler she first must dream. Only then does a weaver know how to combine all the separate designs into one unified pattern.

As Angela drifted off to sleep each night, she would imagine herself standing in the church before the weavers' saint, whispering the weavers' prayer. Every morning she tried hard to reconstruct her dreams, but none of them inspired her later when she sat down at her loom.

One night a hard rain fell. Thunder and lightning disturbed others in the house but Angela slept soundly. She dreamed of colorful butterflies that awoke as the sun rose above the sacred mountain. They fluttered from one corn plant to the next, becoming more and more active as the sun shone more brightly.

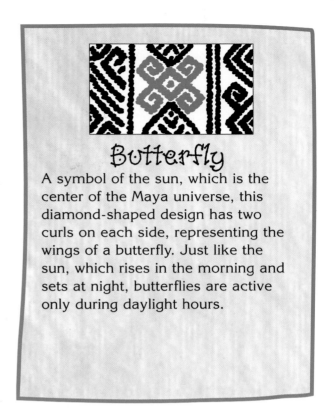

Butterfly

A symbol of the sun, which is the center of the Maya universe, this diamond-shaped design has two curls on each side, representing the wings of a butterfly. Just like the sun, which rises in the morning and sets at night, butterflies are active only during daylight hours.

Snakes slithered along the ground of the milpa. Scorpions scampered from beneath rocks and back into hiding again. The clouds over the sacred mountain turned from white to gray. Toads could be heard singing and a soft rain began to fall. As raindrops struck the earth, the corn—and what seemed like the whole universe—burst into flower.

(Above) Although Angela would prefer to devote all her time to working on her sampler, she has other responsibilities. Sometimes Angela attends school, but teachers are scarce in such rural areas. In the tradition of her people, Angela must work in the house and take care of the small animals her family keeps.

(Right) Angela grinds corn that has been soaked in water and limestone powder overnight. She shapes the cornmeal into perfectly round tortillas. These are cooked over an open fire and are usually eaten with mashed beans and salt.

The next morning, Angela knew she was ready to weave her first sampler. She waited patiently for everyone except Abuelita to leave the house and then blurted out every detail of her dream. Abuelita left the dishes unwashed, and she and Angela hurried to visit Santa Rosario, the weavers' saint, together.

After finishing the prayers, they made a list of the things to be done before Angela could begin her sampler for the contest. The first task was to construct the loom. Angela was to gather seven perfectly straight sticks and ask Abuelito to carve her two smooth battens. Then she and Abuelita would visit the market and buy the finest white cotton thread for tying the loom together and weaving the white sections of her sampler. Lastly, Angela would need to ask the weavers of San Andrés for a few skeins of colored yarn—mostly red, but a little blue, yellow, orange, and green.

Beginning weavers may provide the sticks and white thread that are used in constructing a loom, but more experienced weavers help beginners put their looms together. Certain weavers are recognized as specialists in "warping" looms, and it is not uncommon for weavers from other villages to seek them out when they are starting a new weaving.

Once all this was accomplished and the loom constructed, Angela set to work on her sampler. Every spare moment she could steal from her daily chores, she hung her loom from a post in the yard and wove and wove. Angela's arms stretched, her body swayed, her fingers flew—even when she had to carefully count the pairs of white threads that would go over and under the colored yarns. Even so, it was a long, slow process.

Some evenings as the sun closed in upon the horizon and the shadows crept nearer and nearer, she would stay at her loom, desperate to complete one more row. No one could convince her to come in from the cold. Should she change the pattern? Use fewer designs? Abuelita encouraged her to be patient and stick to her original plan. A weaving must not be rushed; she might brocade no more than an inch a day. The weaver who works slowly and carefully will be rewarded—that was her constant advice. Little by little, Angela's sampler resembled the story in her dream. She finished the last few rows by the light of the fire inside the house only the night before the contest. Her back was stiff, her fingers were sore, but her sampler was ready.

Angela cherishes being left alone in the final days before the contest. She can see the gap decreasing between the woven cloth and the final dowel of the loom. Her entire dream is almost woven into the sampler.

ngela looked around the meadow near the Weavers' House as Abuelita retold the familiar stories. Stews of cabbage and potatoes bubbled in gigantic pots and the smell of warm corn tortillas filled the air. Small groups of weavers and their families shared news with friends from nearby villages. Red, blue, yellow, and white brocaded weavings, waiting for the judges' decisions, brightened the ground and the lines strung between trees. But Angela was much too anxious to enjoy the food, the music, or any of the other festivities.

(Above) Angela's finished sampler

(Opposite) Angela and the other contestants anxiously await the decision of the judges.

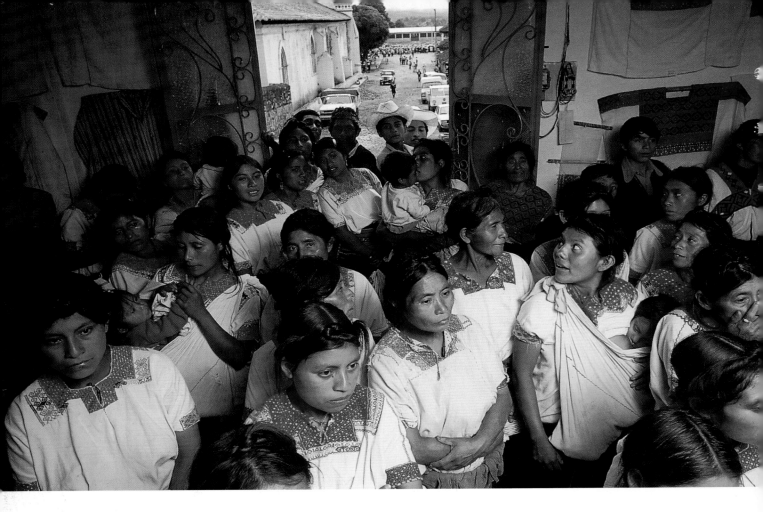

Finally the moment arrived for the First Sampler Prize. All the contestants were called to gather in the Weavers' House. Angela watched as sampler after sampler was held up for the judges. Then they came to hers. One of the judges slowly ran her fingers over the colored designs. Angela could hear her counting the stitches. First row, three under, one over, three under. Next row . . . A second judge pulled at the edges. Not one thread too tight, not one thread too loose. A third judge looked at the combination of designs. Angela could barely watch as the judge tilted her head from side to side, checking the borders as well as the central pattern. Snake, Butterfly, Scorpion, Toad, Ancestors, Universe, Flowering Corn. The judges moved on. After they had examined all of the entries, one of them stepped forward to speak. "The First Sampler Prize goes to Angela. We could not find a single flaw in her work. Her sampler was well dreamt."

(Opposite) All the contestants and their relatives push into the room where the prizes are announced, hoping to catch a glimpse of the award-winning weavings and the weavers who will carry on the village traditions for years to come.

(Above) The First Sampler Prize consists of a cash prize and membership in the Weavers' House.

Fulfilling her promise to Santa Rosario, Angela returns to the church and gives thanks.

Angela could hardly believe what she was hearing. A smile broke out on her face as the applause from the weavers reached her ears. Far in the back of the room she could see the weavers from San Andrés laughing and congratulating Abuelita. Angela pushed her way through the crowd, completely ignoring the hands that reached out in her direction. At last she arrived at Abuelita's side. Beaming, Angela thanked her grandmother for all her help.

Later, Angela would ask her grandmother a final favor—to visit the weavers' saint one more time. There, they would light candles and recite the prayer together. Then they would wash Angela's winning sampler in rose water and hang it on the saint's huipil, fulfilling the promise made so many months before.

As her friends and family gathered around to congratulate her, Angela whispered the weavers' prayer to herself just one more time:

Ak'bun ti oxib ach'ul grasya
Ak'bun ti oxib ach'ul ventisyon
Ti sba yol ajalante'e
Ti sba yol atzutzube
Yu'un la me chak xchan
Yu'un la me chak yich'

Give me three graces
Give me three battens
Give me three heddles
So I may weave my cloth
So I may weave my sampler
So I may one day weave my own huipil.

Glossary

Abuelita   grandma (from the Spanish word *abuela*, meaning "grandmother")

Abuelito   grandpa (from the Spanish word *abuelo*, meaning "grandfather")

Backstrap Loom   Specific type of loom used by Maya weavers. A strap stretches behind the wearer's back and holds one end of the loom. The other end is attached to a pole, a tree, or a hook at some distance from the weaver.

Brocade   A type of weaving where designs are made by inserting the threads as the cloth is being woven, rather than being added to finished cloth.

Carding   A means of cleaning wool by pulling the fibers between two flat combs or brushes with metal bristles to release bits of dirt and straw.

Design   A particular combination and organization of colored threads.

Dyeing   The method of changing or intensifying colors of fibers, such as wool.

Huipil   Traditional blouse or tunic worn by Maya women. It is woven in two rectangular pieces that are stitched together. The designs around the neck and along the sleeve edge identify the town of the woman wearing it and the weaver who produced it.

Master Weaver   Women who have devoted themselves to studying traditional designs and weaving techniques on the layers of huipils decorating the saints of the church or who have learned the craft by apprenticing themselves to older master weavers. They are expected to pass their knowledge on to young weavers and are often the center around which weavers' cooperatives are organized.

Maya   Contemporary indigenous people living in the southern Mexican state of Chiapas as well as the countries of Honduras, Belize, El Salvador, and Guatemala. They speak more than forty languages and are united by ties to the ancient Maya, who flourished from A.D. 100 to A.D. 900. In Chiapas, the Tzotzil Maya live in the western highlands and are a conservative group of villages who maintain the traditions of weaving despite the pressures for change from the modern world.

Metate   A thick smooth stone with a depression in the center. Dried corn kernels are ground in preparation for making tortillas by rolling a second round stone in the depression.

Milpa   cornfield

Sampler   Rectangular piece of cloth woven by Maya girls to practice the designs and to show that they are preparing to become weavers in the village tradition. Women also weave them as demonstrations of their skill or as evidence that they have studied ancient designs on huipils decorating the saints of Maya churches.

Skein   A standard length of yarn measured by winding it around and around outstretched hands.

Spindle   Maya women use a drop spindle, made of a pointed wooden dowel pushed through a flat wooden or clay cylinder. They come in two sizes, a small one for spinning single strands of yarn and a larger one for spinning several strands together.

Spinning   The process of twisting wool fibers into yarn. Spinning is done by stretching a thick strand of wool fibers between a spindle in one hand and a clump of wool fibers in the other. Then the spindle is rotated on the ground, in a ceramic dish or half a dried gourd, which twists the fibers into yarn. The yarn is then wound into a ball at the base of the spindle.

Symbol   A widely recognized representation of a figure.

Bibliography

Morris, Walter F., Jr., and Jeffrey J. Foxx. *Living Maya*. New York: Harry N. Abrams, Inc., 1987.

Tedlock, Dennis, translator. *Popol Vuh*. New York: Touchstone, 1985.

The Maya Territory

At the height of their development, around A.D. 250, the Maya occupied an area of approximately 120,000 square miles (311,000 square kilometers). The region included parts of present-day Mexico (the states of Campeche, Yucatán, and Quintana Roo and part of the states of Tabasco and Chiapas), as well as parts of Guatemala, Honduras, and El Salvador and all of Belize. Today the Maya still live in these countries, but primarily in Guatemala. San Andrés, where Angela lives, is a small town in the Mexican state Chiapas and is not often included on maps. An easier point of reference is San Cristóbal.

The area in yellow on the top map shows the original Maya territory.

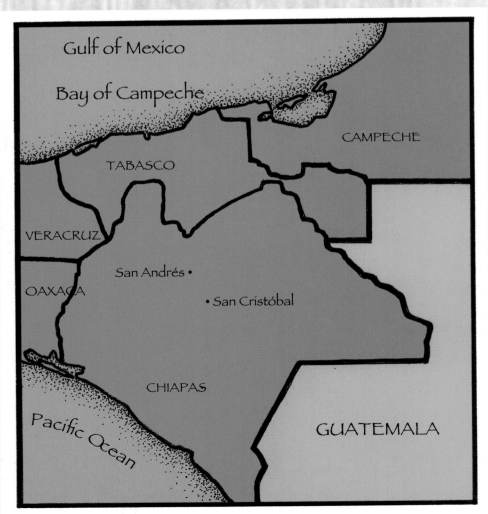

Photographer's Note

I traveled by van to San Andrés, Larrainzar, in the state of Chiapas, Mexico, in search of adventure, beauty, and mystery. And I found it! Although I have made the trip many times now and have good friends there, it still seems incredible that the street in front of my house in Brooklyn, New York, is connected to the street in front of Angela's.

The Maya have lived in Mesoamerica for more than 3,000 years, but their greatest period of development began around A.D. 250 and continued for the next 600 years or so. They built fantastic cities of stone that rose above the jungle, carved their history into stone glyphs, laid fine roads, developed a highly sophisticated system of commerce, created an accurate calendar, constructed observatories to watch the stars, and invented the concept of zero.

Weaving is *the* art form of the modern-day Maya. Try to imagine what you would look like if you had to wear clothes you made by yourself! In Angela's world, people take the wool from the sheep and go through all the processes described in this book. We, on the other hand, live in a store-bought world. When you need new clothes for school or play, you go to the store and buy them. Angela's world is mostly handmade: houses, doors, chairs, beds, fireplaces, shoes, tools—and of course clothes.

However, Angela's world is changing. The international demand for Maya textiles such as woven cloth is in its infancy. As the Maya sell more of their manufactured goods, they, too, are buying foreign products, like radios and sneakers. Slowly the lifestyle that we know is being introduced into their lives. But at the same time, many Maya wish to keep their traditional ways. This collaboration was born in tribute to the Maya. And in the hope that their ancient art form of weaving may be kept alive.

Author's Note

In 1988, the Rockefeller Foundation granted me a Fellowship for Foreign Language Teachers to spend two months in Chiapas, Mexico, and create curricula based on Maya children learning to weave. Pedro Meza of Sna Jolobil (*the Weavers' House*) guided me through much of my two-month stay. He introduced me to master weavers and young girls who were learning the stories and skills of the craft. Angela was one of those girls, and her family was willing to be photographed and have her progress documented. They hoped that other children would learn from the record of Angela's experience.

Angela's story and my collection of weavings created by or worn by Maya children continues to inspire me year after year. In writing *Angela Weaves a Dream*, I have drawn on my classroom explorations with my students at Manhattan Country School as well as my periodic conversations with "Chip" Morris, Pedro Meza, and Lynn Haroldson, to whom I am deeply grateful.

I would like to thank my mother and grandmother, who taught me the value of making beautiful things with my hands; Gary, who is the ultimate lover of good stories; and my father. I also thank Adrian, an avid student of indigenous cultures and a devoted husband.

For Andrea and Caitlin
—M. S.

My effort is dedicated to universal appreciation of all
the "Angelas" and Maya weavers young and old.
Special thanks to Pedro Meza and the weavers'
cooperative Sna Jolobil in San Cristóbal de las Casas,
Chiapas, Mexico.

—J. J. F.

Printed in Hong Kong by South China Printing Company (1988) Ltd.

FIRST EDITION
10 9 8 7 6 5 4 3 2 1

Library of Congress Cataloging-in-Publication Data

Solá, Michèle
    Angela weaves a dream / Michèle Solá ; photographs by Jeffrey Jay
  Foxx —1st ed.
      p.   cm.
    ISBN 0-7868-0073-9 (trade)—ISBN 0-7868-2060-8 (lib. bdg.)
     1. Maya textile fabrics—Juvenile literature. 2. Hand weaving—Mexico—Juvenile literature.
3. Maya mythology—Juvenile literature. 4. Mayas—Social life and customs—Juvenile literature.
    [1. Maya textile fabrics—Juvenile literature. 2. Mayas—Social life and customs. 3. Indians of Mexico—
Social life and customs. 4. Weaving.] I. Foxx, Jeffrey J. (Jeffrey Jay), ill. II. Title.
F1435.3.T48S65   1996
   746.1'4'089974—dc20   94-35488